"Make the Bear Be Nice"

This title is number six in the Frayed Edge Press Street Smart Series

Other titles in the series include:

Full Fare by Jean-Bernard Pouy

Down and Out in Paris, with Cat by R.A. Bolo

The Accidental Anarchist by A.R. Melnik

Stealing MacGuffin by Matthew Kastel

Pele's Domain by Albert Tucher

The Day is Gone by Shelonda Montgomery

"Make the Bear Be Nice"

Stephen St. Francis Decky

Frayed Edge Press
Philadelphia, PA

Copyright 2021

Published by Frayed Edge Press in 2021

https://www.frayededgepress.com/

This book is printed on acid-free paper

Illustrations by Bruce Orr

Publisher's Cataloging-in-Publication Data
Names: Decky, Stephen St. Francis.
Title: "Make the bear be nice" / Stephen St. Francis Decky.
Description: Philadelphia, PA : Frayed Edge Press, 2019. | Series: Street smart
    series ; 6 | Summary: A homeless teen who works cleaning movie theaters has his
    life turned upside down by a couple of unlikely friendships and a chaotic
    uprising during a screening of an annoyingly ubiquitous summer blockbuster
    kids' movie.
Identifiers: LCCN 2021944728 | ISBN 9781642510379 (pbk.) | ISBN
    9781642510386 (ebook)
Subjects: LCSH: Fathers and sons -- Fiction. | Friendship -- Fiction. | Motion
    picture theaters -- Employees -- Fiction. | Young men -- Fiction. | BISAC:
    FICTION / Coming of Age. | FICTION / Family Life / General. | FICTION
    / Friendship.
Classification: LCC PS3604 E25 M35 2021 | DDC 813 D43--dc23
LC record available at https://lccn.loc.gov/2021944728

My job is cleaning the theaters at the Deptford Super-6 Multi-Plex Cinema in Deptford, New Jersey. I do it seven nights a week because I'm trying to save enough money to get my own apartment. Right now, I am not living anywhere.

Cleaning theaters can be gross but it's kinda neat being alone in such a huge place all night. Plus, I actually like cleaning. When I was still living at home, I spent at least an hour every night cleaning something — the bathroom or the living room or the kitchen, which was always a mess because my dad is such a slob. I didn't get paid anything for cleaning at home, but at the movie theater, I get nine dollars an hour. Because there's nobody to supervise me at night, I get paid for eight hours no matter what, even though I usually finish everything up in less than four. I spend the rest of the time sleeping on one of the couches in the lobby. They're very soft and way more comfortable than the backseat of my car.

In the daytime I drink coffee and drive around. Sometimes I buy CDs to play in the car but I'm trying not to spend too much money so if I can, I just steal them. I also steal food.

❧❦

It was three months ago that I got kicked out of my house. The last night I was there, my dad grabbed my neck and

1

slammed me against the wall in my room. He was only wearing his underwear when he did this. He was so mad and the room was kinda dark but the reflection of the light from the hallway made his eyes glow orange.

"I'LL FUCKIN' KILL YOU" is the very last thing he said to me.

I spent the next couple of days wandering aimlessly and feeling terrible but then I got the job at the movie theater and right away I started feeling better—mostly because it meant I was making money but also secretly because I finally had something to clean again.

——

Sometimes in the daytime I see Jimmy Kirkos. He's a waiter at the Freeway Diner and I knew him in high school but we were never friends back then. We're sorta friends now, I think.

"How's the movie business?" he asks me today.

"Kinda messy," I tell him.

He's on his break and sitting in the booth across from me. We've both got coffees and grilled cheese sandwiches.

"Must be cool workin' with no boss around," he says, raising his eyebrows. "Betcha could have a pretty decent party."

"Oh, but I couldn't. I'd get in trouble." I take a bite of my sandwich and wait until I'm done chewing it to say: "Besides, it's been way too busy lately."

The reason it's busy is because it's summer and there's a lotta kids' movies out. All the theaters showing kids' movies are extra messy, and it takes me a little longer every night to get done. I tell Jimmy this, then add, "It's gonna be even worse when *Make the Bear Be Nice* comes out."

"Christ, that friggin' bear," Jimmy grumbles.

There's been a lotta hype about *Make the Bear Be Nice*—it's supposed to be the biggest summer kids' movie ever, and there are posters and signs and ads for it everywhere. People have been talking about it for months and everybody knows the plot: It's about a girl who finds a cuddly bear in the woods and brings it to her house. He is very nice but can't help accidentally knocking shit over and breaking things so her dad gives her an ultimatum: *"Make the bear be nice, or he's out."* The bear in the ads is *really* cute.

"I wonder if it's gonna be good," I say to Jimmy.

"You're fuckin' kiddin', right?" Jimmy replies. "It's gonna be total shit. It don't matter though, it's gonna make a fuckin' kabillion dollars no matter what. Ya know why?" He stops to light a cigarette, then says: "I'll tell ya why. It's because people are fuckin' *dumb*."

"Maybe it won't be all that bad," I say.

"Yeah, right."

When his break is over, I finish my coffee and pay the bill. I'm just getting into my car when I hear somebody call my name. I look up, and Jimmy is standing on the steps outside the diner.

"Hey, gimme a call some night, will ya? We'll go get hammered."

"Alright," I say, even though I don't have his number.

₧₨

The next few days are kinda busy at the theater. In spite of this, I break my all-time FASTEST-CLEANING RECORD on Tuesday night by finishing in just under two hours and fifty-eight minutes. That's including the extra mess from the two kids' movies playing—*The Look-Ups* and *Prince Kebby's*

Castle—as well as spraying the windows and changing all the urinal cakes in the men's room. I sleep soundly in the lobby all through the week, but on Friday I wake up all of a sudden when I hear a car pull into the parking lot and stop right outside the window.

Instinctively, I grab a broom and start sweeping out a spot at the corner of the lobby, just under one of several giant *Make the Bear Be Nice* posters. There's a jangle of keys in the front door and the manager, Miss Ellie, walks in.

"You're still here?" she asks.

I have no idea what time it is and my head's foggy from sleeping so I can only nod.

"You're gonna have to pick up the pace startin' tonight," she says, shaking her head, which makes her many earrings jingle. "*Make the Bear Be Nice* is gonna show in Theaters 1 through 4, and we're adding on late shows to play in all 6 theaters over the weekend. They won't be letting out 'til 1:15 so you're gonna get a late start."

"I can do it."

"I hope you can," she says. "You've been doin' good work and I'm counting on you to make sure the place looks nice, no matter how nasty it gets. And believe me, it ain't gonna be pretty." She pokes my chest with her index finger then adds: "Make sure you get lotsa rest."

"I will."

She nods. "I'm gonna write you in for an extra two hours every night this week—as long as you keep up the good work." She waves one of her many ring-covered fingers at me then starts walking across the lobby. "Now finish up and get the hell outta here."

"Yes, Miss Ellie."

I wait until I hear her go through the door to the office at the end of the hallway before throwing my broom in the closet. I usually take a couple minutes to wash myself up and brush my teeth in the men's room, but there's no way I can do it today. I leave the theater feeling tired and gross.

When I pass the clock on the bank at the end of Multiplex Road, I see that it's only 10:09 a.m., and because I have absolutely nowhere to go and nothing to do, I stop at the store and buy a paper to see what movies are playing in the city.

⁖⁍

It's a long day and I spend most of it walking around and wishing I had an apartment. I would not need a big one or a lot of furniture: Only a chair and a desk and a real bed to sleep in. After living there for a while, I could probably have a bookshelf and maybe a kitchen table.

When my legs start to hurt, I buy a ticket to see the new Dracula movie that's playing everywhere but I fall asleep during the previews. When I wake up, Dracula is telepathically making some poor guy pull off another guy's head so I close my eyes and conk back out to the sound of the people behind me saying *"Oh my gahd"* and *"What the fahhhck"* over and over.

All the lights are on when I wake up again. There's an usher walking up the aisle and gathering trash so I make to get up so I can move out of his way.

"Relax," he says, waving his hand. "Stick around if ya want, next one's startin' in ten minutes."

"Oh, OK, thanks."

I stay awake to watch the movie this time but it's not all that good so I leave in the middle of it and walk to a bar on the corner. I'm not really old enough to buy drinks but the bartender doesn't ask me for ID so after ordering a grilled cheese sandwich I also ask for a beer. He brings it to me and I drink it. It's pretty good.

By the time I finally get to my car and start heading back over the bridge it's almost midnight. Because of the late shows I won't be able to start work yet so I stop at the Freeway Diner and am surprised to see Jimmy is working because he usually only works in the daytime. The place is packed.

"Gonna have to sit at the counter," he says to me, frowning. "We been packed all day—*'cuz a that fuckin' bear.* I'm on double-overtime."

There are a pair of old-lady waitresses working and one of them brings me a coffee, which is all I want. It would be nice to talk to Jimmy, but because he's so busy it's just not gonna happen. It's not until I've finished my third cup and the clock on the wall across from me says it's 1:15 on the dot that I stand up.

Jimmy follows me to the door. He rips a page out of his checkbook and hands it to me. There's a phone number written on it.

"Whenever you wanna get fucked up," he says.

"OK, sure," I tell him.

He winks and I leave.

❧ ❧

There are still cars in the parking lot when I get to the theater but I wait until the last of the employees leaves before getting out and using my key to get in. The first thing I see is a giant Make the Bear Be Nice standee by the window, which wasn't there when I left this morning. The bear's arm is moving back and forth and every once in a while, his eyes light up and turn sorta yellow. The trashcan beside him has been overturned; popcorn boxes and soda cups are spread out all around it. The carpet is totally covered with trash and stains for as far as I can see. I walk through it really slow because I've never seen such a mess in my whole life.

The theaters are much, much worse. I go through every one of them with my mouth open and my head shaking back and forth, with posters and signs for *Make the Bear Be Nice* flashing all around me.

"It's impossible" is alls I can think.

There's no time to waste at all so I literally run to the broom closet and get out the leaf-blower, which is what you use to blow all the trash in the theaters to the front. It's the first time I've ever had to use it on the lobby and that's not a good sign. By the time I've gotten to the theaters it's already closing in on 4 a.m.

"There's no way you can stop," I tell myself. *"You have to work harder than you've ever worked before, AND YOU CANNOT STOP 'TIL IT'S ALL DONE."*

For the next five hours, I am sweating and coughing all over the place from the dust and dirt blown up by the leaf-blower. The theaters get worse as I go along: there's candy stuck to half the seats and pools of spilled soda everywhere. Theater 4 smells like vomit and it's not until I go to wipe off a seat with a rag and hit a big chunky wet spot that I find out why. I have to run to the men's room when this happens and I waste two precious minutes washing my hands and trying to think of nice things to keep myself from barfing.

But in the end, I get the job done. The dumpster outside is filled to capacity so I'm hoping the trashmen come today to empty it. I am just climbing into my car when I see Miss Ellie's car pull in off of Multiplex Road and speed toward her parking spot, which has a special sign in front of it that reads *RESERVED FOR MANAGER.*

...I am sweating and coughing all over the place from the dust and dirt blown up by the leaf-blower. The theaters get worse as I go along...

॥

This day is even longer than yesterday because I'm totally exhausted and there's nowhere to sleep. I try parking in the lot of my old high school, but even though I'm buried under dirty clothes in the backseat some kids spot me and start pushing the car back and forth until it feels like it might tip over. They are giving me the finger when I drive away and although I want to tell them they might die alone and in agony someday, I just drive away instead.

I'm too tired to go to the city so I get a coffee to go from Burger Dan's on Route 41 before heading to the local Shopper's Paradise Supermarket to steal some food.

I'm shoving a bag of cookies into my pants when my dad walks into the aisle.

It's too late to pull the bag out and I'm too confused to run, so I just stand there 'til he looks up and notices me.

"Yo," he says, nodding his head and trying to look tough with a shopping basket fulla toilet paper in his hand. "The hella you doin' here?"

"Shoppin'," I say.

"No shit? Where you livin' these days?"

"At my friend's house," I say.

"Oh yeah?" His eyes look funny under the bright fluorescent lights and even though I want to I can't turn away from them. "What friend? You ain't got any friends—I know that."

"I'm stayin' at Jimmy Kirkos' house."

"Jiminy Who? Jiminy Cricket?" He shakes his head. "Hate to tell you this, kid, but Jiminy Cricket's not real—he's a grasshopper in a cartoon."

There is always this feeling around my dad that I'm about to get physically injured. It could be a punch or a shove or both. When I was living at his house this feeling was always there, and no matter how nice I was being or how good I did in school it wouldn't leave.

"I gotta go," I say.

"Where you gotta go?"

He grabs my arm and I stop and close my eyes.

"You ain't goin' nowhere," he tells me. "I seen your car at the movie theater every morning the past coupla months. You think I'm stupid? I pass it every day comin' back from work." I don't want to look at his face, but I do. My eyes start to water. "I want'cha to come home," he continues. "Ya can't hide from me, I'm your dad. I know what you're up to."

"I'm not up to anything. Let go," I say.

"*Let go*," he says, making it sound like I'm a scaredy-cat. I have to push him with my free hand but the motion makes the bag of cookies go *POP!* in my pants and just like that a wave of crumbs is rolling into my underwear and down my legs.

"The fuck was that?" Dad says.

I push him again, with both hands now, and his head bonks against one of the shelves. He shouts some kinda threat, but I can't hear it because I'm crying and running for the front doors with little pieces of cookies and cupcakes and all the other shit I stole spilling outta my pockets and shirt and pants.

� ৫৪

The only other thing to do today is to get as far away as I can so I drive all the way out to where my Aunt Bette lives in Cumberland County and park in the woods across from her house. My legs and belly are itching from all the crumbs down there and even though I know Aunt Bette would be happy to let me use her bathroom to get cleaned up, I'm too embarrassed to knock on her door. I lay down in the backseat and fall asleep scratching myself and every once in a while making a pathetic kind of whimpering lonely animal sound.

When I wake up it's so dark that I can't even see my own hand so I climb up into the front seat and start the car. The clock on the dashboard says 1:20 a.m. and I stare at it for a minute trying to think why this is bad and then I remember I'm thirty minutes away from the theater and already late. I back up out of the woods and drive as fast as I can back to Deptford.

There is no way the theater can be worse than it was yesterday but—amazingly—it is. The trash is piled so high in the lobby that I trip twice before I even reach the hallway. The amount of energy I'm gonna need to do all this is almost impossible to think of so I just stop thinking about it and get to work. *"You cannot mess this up"* is what I keep telling myself, but by the time the sun comes up I'm not even halfway done. My arms are aching so bad I can hardly even hold up the leaf-blower when I reach Theater Six, but it's almost 9 a.m. so I just keep working even though my head is hurting and my legs feel like they're gonna snap off and every once in a while I get such a heavy feeling of sadness that I just wanna stop and melt into the gum and melted gummy-bear-stained carpet.

But there's still no way I'm gonna stop. I just work and right as I'm hauling the last few bags of trash out to the dumpster, I hear the sound of Miss Ellie and the morning crew walking into the lobby to start the next day's work.

₧₧

I'm too tired to drive all the way to Aunt Bette's again so I go to the Freeway Diner and park out back by the dumpster. I'm sleeping in the backseat totally covered up with dirty clothes when the front door opens and somebody climbs in behind the wheel.

My hair's all over the place and my eyes are hardly able to focus, but I know right away it's Jimmy.

"The fucka ya doin'?" he asks. "The manager saw your car out here and wanted to call the cops."

"Sorry," is alls I can say.

"You alright?" He leans back a little to give my face a good look, then says: "You don't look alright. It's that fuckin' movie, ain't it? *Make the Bear Be* DEAD. Fuck." He lights a cigarette, shaking his head back and forth. "Look, man, I wish I could let'cha stay here but my boss is a jackass. This is the first break I had all day and I been on since eight in the mornin'."

"What time is it?"

"Little after two." He leans back and reaches into his pocket then pulls out a set of keys. It takes him a minute but eventually he yanks one of them off of the keyring and holds it toward me. "Here, take this. You know where Almonesson is?"

"Uh-huh."

"Right. I live at the end of Cooper Street, across from the Krazy Kat. There's no driveway or anything, there's just a hole in the sidewalk and a buncha dirt and trees but there's a mailbox at the end with KIRKOS written on it." He pushes the key into my hand. "Just use the key if nobody answers. My sister's there but knowin' her she's prob'ly sleepin' in fronta the TV. I'll try callin' 'er first."

I am clutching the key tight in my hand when Jimmy opens the door and climbs out.

"You'll prob'ly be gone before I get there, so try and stop by tomorrow. Maybe me and you can go out and have a couple drinks, figger out a way to kill that fuckin' bear forever."

He gives me a thumbs-up and closes the door. It takes some effort but eventually I manage to crawl up to the front seat and start the engine. In the rear-view mirror, I can see Jimmy lighting a cigarette while pissing against the dumpster. He throws another thumbs-up as I pass.

❧

I drive past the house three times before I spot the mailbox with KIRKOS written on it. The hole in the sidewalk is so deep that the front end of my car goes *KA-THUNK* and my head bangs against the ceiling when I hit it. The house is small and almost totally hidden by trees. I park right in front of it and get out.

Jimmy's sister is standing in the doorway with the door open. She is short with blonde hair and rolled-up sleeves. She's smoking a cigarette.

"Hey, Buddy," she says. "Jimmy called 'n said ya need a place to rest?"

"Is it OK?" I ask.

"For sure. I'm Robin." She reaches out to shake my hand and for just a second I take it.

Inside the house it's pretty gross. There's beer and soda bottles all over the place and also a smell that's sort of like chicken soup but not really. A TV is on with the volume way up but Robin turns it down with a clunky remote.

"Siddown. You wanna beer?"

Inside the house it's pretty gross. There's beer and soda bottles all over the place and also a smell that's sort of like chicken soup but not really.

"Oh, no thanks."

She is pointing to a couch with all sorts of clothes and bags on it so I push some stuff aside and take a seat. On the TV the Phillies are playing a game against the Mets. There is a break in the game and a commercial for *Make the Bear Be Nice* comes on.

"Jesus, this mothafuckin' bear," Robin says.

There are other chairs in the room but Robin sits down on the couch right next to me. She doesn't smell bad but being close to her makes me realize how bad I stink: It's the same stink you get in a gross movie theater, a syrupy kind of old food smell mixed with sweat and buttery popcorn.

"Do you think I could maybe take a shower?" I ask. I've been making sure to clean myself up every day in the men's room at the theater and I even have a bar of soap and a washcloth hidden under one of the sinks there. In all honesty, though, it's been three months since I've taken a real shower.

"Oh yeah, for sure," Robin says, grabbing a can of beer from the floor and shaking it before taking a sip. "Bathroom's right down the hall. You got clean clothes?"

I have to think a minute before I say, "I don't know. I'll have to look in my car."

"Well, bring all your dirty stuff in," she says. "You can wash it while you're gettin' cleaned up."

"Really?"

"Yeah, we got a washer/dryer in the kitchen. Go 'head, grab your stuff."

She shakes her beer and takes another sip.

Outside, I gather up all the clothes in the backseat and carry them back to the house, feeling like this is all too good to be true.

Robin is waiting at the door.

"Jimmy didn't tell me you were so cute," she says, not really looking at me. "It…could be a problem."

I almost laugh but I hold it in. Robin stretches the door open a little further so I can squeeze through it. Our eyes meet briefly as I pass but I don't know what that means.

⁖⁗

The bathroom smells awful and feels like a TV crime scene. There is pee in the toilet and a black ring around the bathtub. The shower curtain has black stuff all around the bottom of it. When you look up close, the black stuff is wet and fuzzy.

I turn on the water and take off my clothes.

I'm afraid to touch anything while I'm under the water, so I just sorta stand there for a while and let it wash over my hair and skin. There's some pieces of soap at the bottom of the tub and a couple of shampoo bottles, but mostly alls you see is cigarette butts—they're in the soap dish and in the little shower rack and also clogged up in the drain.

I get out of the tub after a couple minutes. All the towels have black stains on them so I use my dirty t-shirt to dry myself. I'm standing in the middle of the bathroom, still dripping all over the place, when the door opens and Robin walks in.

"I'm not gonna look," she says. She's holding a hand up to her face but I can see a little space between her fingers and the watery glitter of her eye behind it. There's a clean towel in her free hand and she's holding it out toward me. I take it and wrap it around my middle.

"Your stuff's in the dryer," she says. "You hungry?"

"A little."

"I'm makin' baked mac 'n cheese. It's in the oven right now but it'll be done in, like, fifteen/twenty minutes." She exhales smoke, but turns her head left so's not to blow it in my face. "Maybe you could take a nap 'til it's done?"

I don't know what to say because I'm more nervous than tired right now, but I can't stand in the filthy bathroom anymore so I follow Robin to a doorway in the middle of the hallway and walk in behind her. There's a kids-size bed pushed up against a wall but no light so it's hard to see anything else except piles of stuff all over the floor.

"I'm not that tired," I say.

"Yeah, right," she tells me, staring right into my eyes with a funny smile. I turn away and look toward the bed, then lean down on it. It's been three months since I slept on a real bed. This one's tiny, but right now it feels voluptuous.

I lay down on it all the way and within seconds I'm out like a light.

ⅎ⅓

When I wake up, I'm struggling to breathe and for a second I feel like it's because I'm having a panic attack but then I realize there's a terrible smell coming from somewhere and when I look out into the hallway alls I see is smoke.

"I think something's burning," I say.

From the living room, I can hear a beer can hit the ground followed by Robin yelling "Ah, shit!"

She stumbles into the kitchen and turns off the oven, which has thick black smoke pumping out of it. My eyes are all watered-up so it's hard to see, but I find the back door and open it before making my way all around the tiny house, tripping over plates and bottles while opening up the windows. I'm still only wearing a towel so when I'm done, I pull my clothes out of the dryer and walk back to the bathroom. The clothes are not completely dry, but it doesn't matter. I get dressed quickly then carry what I'm not wearing out to the car.

It's dark out. I'm teary-eyed and having trouble breathing because of all the smoke. There's the sound of somebody coughing behind me and then Robin comes out through the front door and sits down on the top step.

"Sorry, I conked out on the couch," she says, then coughs again. "I bet if we scrape the burnt parts off, the mac 'n cheese'll still be good. Whaddya think?"

"I gotta go to work."

"Right now?"

I'm standing on the dirt lawn and looking down at her and I'm completely confused. There is one part of me that wants to run away but another part that wants to sit down next to her and tell her stuff, and listen to her tell me stuff. Instead, I just stand there for another minute.

"I know the house is gross," she says. "I'm gonna clean it, eventually. Someday. We've had a lot goin' on here lately, though. I don't know if Jimmy told'ja."

What Jimmy told me was that their mom died a few months ago. It was the thing that made us be friends, I think. My mom died when I was in high school, so I was sort of able to tell how he was feeling.

"We got insurance money from it but Mom's lawyer tried to rip us off, so we had to get another one," she says. "The money's still coming but prolly not 'til September. I'm figuring I'll start cleanin' up toward the end of August."

Alls I can do is nod.

"C'mon, come back inside and have dinner with me," Robin says. "Twenty bucks says you're hungrier than I am." She coughs, then adds: "You're definitely lonelier."

☙❧

The black stuff peels off the top of the mac 'n cheese pretty easily, and although the rest of it's a little dry, it's not bad if you dip it in ketchup. I'm starving anyway so I eat two bowls of it on the back porch while Robin smokes cigarettes and drinks beer in the chair across from me.

"Jimmy talks about you a lot," she says. "I sorta remember you from school but I graduated the year before you and him were seniors. Your hair was always fucked-up and you looked like you were stoned all the time, that's alls I remember."

"I wasn't ever stoned."

"It's what you looked like."

I don't like to think about high school because it wasn't much fun. My mom was sick for a long time and for a long time after she died, I pretty much just wanted to die too. It wasn't until Dad kicked me out of the house and I got the job at the theater that I really felt like I even wanted to be part of the regular world again.

When I'm done eating, I volunteer to do the dishes but doing the dishes only makes me want to clean the kitchen, so I do that, and with Robin's permission, I gather up all the trash from the bedroom and the living room and haul it out to the curb in clunky white trash bags. The entire house still needs to be rubbed down with some kind of de-greaser and vacuumed, but it's getting late and I have to go to work soon.

"I'd love to stay and clean the bathroom," I say, meaning it.

"Come back tomorrow and do it," she says. We are standing in the living room and she is looking at me in a way that's both pleading and confused. "Seriously—come back, OK?"

"For sure," I say.

∞∞

The mess at the theater is impossible to explain; I feel weak and insignificant before it, like I'm having some kinda existential crisis. There's no time for that kinda crap, though. I was running too late to stop by the diner for coffee before work, but I'm so hyped to have taken a shower and eaten a home-cooked meal that I'm able to clean like I've never cleaned before.

It felt kind of energizing to have met Robin too, but I should mention that I don't really like girls. I mean I like them and respect them and like being friends with them, but I don't like them beyond that. I'm not sure I like guys either, but I get the feeling sometimes that later on I might. More importantly, it's been a long time since I had a truly best friend and I would be really interested in having one right now.

The sun is just coming up through the windows in the lobby when I carry out the final trash bag. I go back inside to lock everything up but instead of going out to my car and driving away, I lay down in the lobby and fall asleep with the whirr and grind of the *Make the Bear Be Nice* standee echoing behind me.

∞∞

What wakes me up is the sound of something banging against the window. I stand and grab the broom beside the couch and make like I'm sweeping for a second, but then I stop and look around. The front door is still closed and there's no sign of Miss Ellie.

There's another BANG against the window.

Slowly, I move toward the curtains and pull them apart. What I see is the big round face of my dad staring in at me. He waves for me to come outside.

⁂⁂⁂

"I want'cha to come home," is what he tells me. We're sitting on the curb outside the movie theater and I have no idea what time it is. Alls I know is it's early.

"I'm gettin' an apartment next week," I tell him. It might not be a lie. If my check is as big as I'm hoping it will be, I should probably have enough for a down payment on my own place. When I think about it, I can almost smell it: it will smell clean and nice and also it will be very quiet.

"Oh, so now alla sudden you're all grown up, right?" Dad says. "Gonna get your own apartment and all that. Who the hell's gonna rent a place to you?" He pauses to light a cigarette before adding, "You're just a little friggin' punk."

His car is parked next to mine in the parking lot. Every once in a while, a car passes on Multiplex Road but none of them belong to Miss Ellie.

"I'm not a punk," is what I tell him. "Mom always said I was smart."

It's quiet for a long time and I'm able to think about the house and Dad and how different things have been since

21

Mom died. When she was there, I never thought about leaving; I only thought about going to college and studying to be a teacher, which I think would be a great job for me. But after she was gone, Dad got quiet for a few months and then he turned mean. It wasn't long before the only thing on my mind was running away.

"Alright, you're not a punk," Dad says. "If your mother heard me say that, she'd punch me in the mouth." He shakes his head a little, then huffs out a big smoky breath and adds, "I don't mean to be such a jerkoff. You lost your mom, but I lost my wife. I known her since I was your age and…" He pauses to rub his face. "You just don't know what it's like."

"I need to get my own place," I tell him.

It takes a while for him to respond. "No, you don't," he says. "You got a place; I ain't even stepped foot in your room since you left. I got money in the bank, but I got nothin' to spend it on. I don't even drink anymore; I just work and go to sleep." He puts his hand on my shoulder for a second and I'm scared he's gonna hug me, but instead he just stands up and says, "It's been three years—three years since she died. If she knew how things turned out, she'd…she'd kick me in the friggin' nuts." He crushes out his cigarette before adding: "I'm only tryna say I'm sorry."

I can tell he wants to look me in the eyes, so I just keep staring at my hands which are sticky and red in spots from touching melted candy.

"Whenever you're ready," he says, "you come home. I ain't goin' anywhere else, so you know where to find me."

When I look up his eyes are all bloodshot and watery. We stare at each other for a second and then his hand comes out toward me. I have just reached out to shake it when Miss Ellie's car pulls into the lot.

ഇൻ

I drive out to the woods across from Aunt Bette's house and sleep until it's dark. There's still plenty of time before I have to get back to the theater, so I drive to Jimmy's house to see if Robin might want to get dinner. The front door is open and I can see her drinking beer on the couch.

"Come in," she says. "I was thinking of you earlier so I went out and bought all kindsa cleanin' stuff."

This is without a doubt the most thoughtful thing anyone's done for me in a long time.

"There's some bread and cheese and stuff if you wanna make a sandwich," she adds.

"Oh yeah? I'm pretty hungry — I could prob'ly eat three of 'em."

Together, we finish half a loaf of bread and all the cheese in the fridge. When we're done, we go through everything she got at the grocery store, which feels like genuine treasure: there's a big bottle of Colonel Pine's Pine-Scented All-Purpose Cleanser, a 12-pack of Generally Nice Brand paper towels, a Bonus-Pack of Jonny-Sponge rainbow-colored sponges, and a couple more bags full of bathroom, kitchen, and multi-use cleaning supplies and implements. Together, we start scrubbing down the kitchen, though after a few minutes Robin sort of sits down on the kitchen table, smoking a steady stream of cigarettes while I continue cleaning. It's a long time before either of us says anything, but in between our eyes meet a couple times and I smile a little and so does she.

ഇൻ

I head off to work a little later, and as I'm pulling into the diner for some coffee, I realize I haven't seen Jimmy since he gave me the key to his house. He nods to me when I step inside and joins me at a booth a few minutes later.

"So what's it like fuckin' my sister?" is the first thing he says to me.

Jimmy's eyes are red and there is sweat all over his arms and hands. He has been working for fourteen hours straight but he doesn't look tired at all: he looks insane.

"That definitely didn't happen," I say.

"Liar."

He winks and slurps from the coffee cup in front of him.

"I'm serious," I say. "She's pretty cool, though."

"I know," Jimmy says. "I'm just ridin' ya. I know you're a decent kid, you ain't like that. The problem is girls are animals. Guys like me an' you don't have a chance against 'em. If you got money, they'll take it. If you ain't got that, they'll just take somethin' else—your balls or your brains or both. It's a scientific fact: *Girls make you dumb.* Look it up."

I'm not sure where Jimmy got this information from and I definitely don't agree with it but I nod anyway, mostly because he looks even more bonkers than usual.

"Look, Robin's a goofball but she's my sister and I love 'er." He looks me square in the eye then adds: "Don't get 'er upset, OK? We been through a lot this year."

"I definitely won't."

He is taking another slurp of his coffee when a man with a gigantic moustache leans out of the kitchen and says, "Hey Jimmy, break over." He disappears before he can see Jimmy holding up his middle finger.

"I'm gonna wrap a fuckin' plate around somebody's face tonight, just wait," he says. "We'll talk later."

He gets up and puts his apron on but I stay in the booth to finish my coffee, which tastes really refreshing and nice.

❧

When I get done work in the morning I drive to the mall and steal some CDs then listen to them while driving to Glendora. As I'm turning onto my old street, I realize that this is the first time I've been this close to the house since Dad kicked me out. I was only meaning to drive past it—just to see if it still looks the same—but when I see his car is not in the driveway I pull up in front of the curb and just sit there for a minute with the engine still running. The lawn has not been mowed all summer and the grass looks like a jungle, with burnt patches spread out all over it. The little flower garden beside the steps is totally overrun with weeds and there is a giant wasp nest hanging down next to the gutter near the driveway.

I turn off the engine and get out of the car, heading straight for the garden.

Half an hour later, I'm still kneeling in the dirt with my hands all dried-out and black and I'm sweating from the heat of the sun on my head. It takes almost two hours to finish pulling all the weeds. When I'm done, I grab the hose from the side of the house and give the whole garden a good watering because I know there are still flowers in there somewhere.

After taking a long drink from the hose, I walk to the backyard and pull the lawnmower from the shed. The gas tank is more than half-full and the engine starts on the first pull. It takes a while to get through the backyard because there are a lot of rocks beneath the grass and they keep getting caught and shutting down the engine. Also, one of them flies out and hits me right in the balls, and for a second it feels like I got stabbed with a knife there. I step behind the shed for a quick exam and everything looks alright, but it still aches a little.

I check the clock on my dashboard when I'm done with the front lawn and am surprised by how much time has passed: It's almost three o'clock, and my entire body is coated with a film of dirt and sweat. I take another drink from the hose then give the grass a good watering before climbing back into my car. For a while, I just stare at the house, because it would be nice to go inside and take a shower but even though I still have a key—it's jingling right there on my keyring right now—there's no way I'm ever gonna step into that house again.

⬥⬥⬥

There is no answer at Robin's house and I'm about to walk back to my car when the door suddenly opens and she is there. Only one of her eyes is open and there is a sheet covered with pictures of giraffes wrapped around her.

"Were you, like, rollin' around in a dumpster?" she asks.

"I mowed my dad's lawn," I tell her.

She yawns and says, "I was up 'til like nine this mornin'. Jimmy freaked out and kicked a hole in the wall last night and then we just sat around drinkin' 'til he had to go to work."

"You want me to come back later?"

"No, stay here. Take a shower and then come talk with me on the back porch."

I say "Alright" and then follow her into the house.

There is no way I can take a shower until the bathtub is cleaned so I fill the tub with hot water and bleach and throw the shower curtain into it. While it's soaking, I scrub out the toilet and clean the walls and mirrors, then sweep out all the trash that's gathered on the floor. When I'm finished mopping, I drain the tub and scrub it. All the nasty stains are gone from the shower curtain, and by the time I step into the shower and turn on the water, the whole bathroom looks and smells like new.

⁗⁗⁗

It's almost eight o'clock when my stomach starts growling from hunger. We are sitting on the back porch and Robin is smoking a cigarette.

"Dude, you gotta start eatin' more regular," she says, tapping my belly. "That thing's tryna tell you somethin'."

"Maybe we could go out somewhere?" I say.

"That's cool, except I gotta bring Jimmy's car to the diner. I drove him in this morning, he was too fuckin' drunk to drive."

I shake my head.

Robin says, "You prob'ly think I'm a lazy bum but the thing is I don't need a job right now—what I need is time to think. I want the next part of my life to be better than the last part, and I got this time right now to think about how I'm gonna make that happen." She taps out her cigarette, then adds: "Anyway, things are gonna change once that money comes."

"I totally never thought you were a bum."

"I know it, and I know I don't need to tell *you* this, but I got nothin' to hide and I don't need any judgment."

I nod because losing somebody affects everybody different and even after all this time, I still don't know how to put it into words.

It's almost a full minute later when I ask: "If youse got money comin' why is Jimmy working so much?"

"It's 'cuz he's *fucking nuts.* I don't mind that part, though— there's no way I'd be able to live here if he wasn't gone half the day." She fakes a shiver, then adds: "Soon as we get that money though, I'm gettin' my own place. Nothin' fancy, ya know? Just a place in like Woodbury or Haddon Heights, somewhere I feel good and safe and can think about what I'm gonna do next."

"That's almost exactly how I feel about living right now," I tell her, and it's the truth.

"Maybe we could find a place together?" she says.

It takes me a minute but after thinking about it I tell her: "No, I don't think that's a good idea. Not now."

"But we could live somewhere close," she says.

"Yeah," I say. "I can picture that."

∞

We could go almost anywhere to eat but because the diner is so close and Robin has to bring the car there, it's where we go. We get fries and grilled cheese sandwiches and we're almost finished when Jimmy sits down next to Robin and pours the entire contents of a small bottle of Yukon Jack into a glass. He winks and taps the glass against my coffee cup then takes a drink.

"Look, I got a plan," he says. "I been thinkin' about it all day. I was gonna do it myself but since youse are here, maybe we could all do it together."

"Do what?" Robin asks.

I look at Robin who looks at Jimmy who nods at both of us and smiles.

"I wanna go to the movies," he says. "There's a 9:30 show—if we leave in like fifteen minutes, we could definitely make it."

"What movie?" I ask.

"Dude," Jimmy says. "You know what movie."

Robin starts shaking her head right away. "No, no, no, no fuckin' way," she says. "There's no way I'm payin' to see that stupid bear."

There is saliva hanging out of both sides of Jimmy's mouth and his hair is totally slick with sweat. His eyes are bulging and staring into my face. He leans forward a little.

"I think I can get us in for free," is alls I can say.

∞∞∞

The line for tickets is very long, so I lead Jimmy and Robin around to the back of the theater and use my key to get in through the entrance behind the dumpster. This opens up into the front of Theater Six, so we sneak out into the hallway and down to Theater 4. There are no ushers around and because the place is so packed, nobody really notices us.

The movie is not very good. The story is so flat you can pretty much tell what every actor's gonna say before they even say it. Still, the crowd seems enchanted, and when the bear tells the girl he's sorry for blowing up the washing machine and that he loves her, you can even hear some kids start to cry.

There is saliva hanging out of both sides of Jimmy's mouth and his hair is totally slick with sweat. His eyes are bulging and staring into my face. He leans forward a little.

Jimmy is sitting to my left and groaning out loud through most of the movie. Every once in a while, somebody turns around and says "Shhh!" but Jimmy just gives them the finger or tells them to buzz off. Robin is on my right and every time Jimmy says something I can feel her tense up.

We are a little over an hour into the movie when, pretty much outta nowhere, Jimmy says, loudly: "Fuck you, Bear."

On the screen, the girl's dad is pointing at the bear and yelling. The bear's eyes are all moist and the little girl is holding his hand. Inside the theater, several people have turned around to look at us.

"THE FUCKA YOU LOOKIN' AT?" Jimmy yells at them. "I AIN'T TALKIN' TO YOU—I'M TALKIN' TO THE BEAR."

A man right in front of us stands suddenly, blocking out the screen. There are kids on both sides of him and they are both crying and shouting "DADDY, NOOOO!"

"Listen," the man says, waving his finger in Jimmy's face. "I've had just about enough of you—"

Jimmy grabs the finger and twists it up.

There is a snapping sound and right after that, the man lets out a howl that makes the whole theater erupt in nervous chaos; some people begin running for the doors while others yell for everyone to shut up and calm down.

Jimmy stands and pushes the man in front of us to the floor, which knocks the giant tub of popcorn on his armrest into the air, spraying popcorn everywhere. I try to grab Jimmy's arm but he pushes me aside and grabs a giant-sized cup of soda from the seat next to him then hurls it at the screen. The bear is just hopping onto a bicycle and riding away from the house when the soda hits: It makes a thunderous

SPLASH! but on top of that you can hear everybody in the crowd shouting "NO!" and "STOP IT!"

There is soda spilling all down the bear's face when he crashes into a tree and starts to cry.

"YOU FUCKIN' PEOPLE ARE IDIOTS," Jimmy hollers above everything, and with real sincerity in his voice. "THIS IS THE STUPIDEST FUCKIN' MOVIE EVER MADE, AND YOU *KNOW* IT!"

He's in the aisle now, and the light from the screen gives a clear view of his silhouette reaching in toward the seats and knocking buckets of popcorn all over the floor. A few people try to grab him but he only shoves them away.

"FUCK THE BEAR!" he screams above all the other screams. "MAKE THE BEAR GET FUCKED! YOU GUYS ARE SUCH FUCKIN' IDIOTS!"

He is all the way up in the front of the theater now, jumping up at the screen and banging his fists against it. I'm kind of in shock and also scared that I might get in trouble because I helped Jimmy get in for free, but at the same time it's pretty dark in here and everyone is pretty much in shadow. Plus, there's just so many people and it's hard to move until all of a sudden I feel Robin pulling at my arm and the next thing I know we are both running down the aisle toward the screen. By this time the entire audience is on their feet and several people are trying to pull Jimmy to the ground. He throws some punches then grabs somebody's arm and bites it.

There is blood all over his face and his fists when Robin grabs him from behind and starts pulling him toward the front EXIT. I'm right behind her, holding onto her shirt, and I have to use my elbows and also kick some people to keep them from stopping us.

As soon as we're outside, I start running around the building toward the parking lot. Jimmy is screaming "DIE MOTHERFUCKER" over and over, but it's Robin's hand I feel on my arm as we turn the corner and make a beeline to my car.

Jimmy is still screaming when I start the engine and screech out toward Multiplex Road.

☙❧

It feels like a lot of time has passed but it's really only just after eleven when I pull into the dirt outside of Jimmy's house. He's not screaming anymore but he's mumbling and crying and when me and Robin try dragging him into the house, he bites my leg and kicks Robin in the chest so we just leave him in the dirt and go inside.

"You see that?" she says. She's nodding out toward the driveway as she shakes a can of beer sitting on top of the TV. "That happens three, four times a week. I mean it's not always at the movies or in public? But there's always something he's goin' over the top about. When Mom was still here, she used to punch him—I mean she'd just like haul off and punch him in the face. Sometimes it knocked him out cold." She takes a drink from the can and tells me: "Maybe that's what it is—maybe he got brain damage from all them punchouts."

I'm almost scared to leave her alone when it's time to go to work, but Robin says it's alright. She locks the door as soon as as I'm out.

When I get to the car, Jimmy is still lying beside it.

"Jimmy," I say.

One of his eyes opens but he doesn't say anything. It's a little chilly out and I can't just leave him here in the dirt, so I

33

half-lift, half-drag him onto the porch then cover him with a blanket from my back seat.

There are a pair of police cars in the parking lot at the theater when I arrive, so I park near the back of the lot and walk toward the front door. Miss Ellie is standing outside with her hands on her hips and a big frown on her face. She asks me if I know anything about what happened at the 9:30 showing of *Make the Bear be Nice* but I tell her "No."

"The screen in Theater 4 is wrecked," she tells me. There's a cop standing right behind her and although I should be scared, I'm not. "Just clean it up like you usually do, but leave the screen alone. We'll have to see about getting a new one this week." She looks pale and sick and when she puts her hand on my shoulder, I jump a little. "This whole fuckin' bear thing has been a nightmare," she tells me.

Alls I can do is nod. The cop behind her starts asking her questions, so I walk down the hallway and pull the leaf-blower out of the closet. As far as I'm concerned, it's time to get to work.

ꙮ

The cops linger for another hour or so, but by the time I've got the first three theaters cleaned up, the place is empty. In the morning, I drive to a convenience store on Route 41 and carry a pair of coffees back out to the car. I also buy a newspaper, and am not surprised to find the incident at the movie theater reported on the front of the Local News section.

Jimmy is still on the porch, curled up in the blanket when I pull into the driveway.

"What time's it?" he asks.

"Almost eight."

"I'm late for work."

"I can drive you there if you want," I say, "but it might be better if you just call in sick."

I tell him about the story in the newspaper: What it says is that there will be an official investigation and that if anybody knows anything about what happened, they should call the Deptford Police.

"Fuckit," he says, taking a sip of the coffee while rubbing his head. "Fuck the fuckin' diner, I quit. I shoulda quit a long time ago."

"Maybe you oughta take a vacation," I tell him. "Just a couple days, ya know? You could go to the beach."

"Maybe, yeah," he replies. "You're right, I should take a break. I think I'm tryna kill myself."

"You don't deserve that."

"You're right. I don't."

I help him stand up. He's weaving a little, so I help him with his housekey and hold him tight as I push the door open. The sound of Robin snoring from the little bedroom echoes through the house.

Jimmy stomps toward the couch and flops down onto it.

"I got another plan," he says, pointing his finger toward the ceiling. "If that movie's still out when I get back? I'm gonna rent a bear-suit and stand outside the theater. When the kids come up to shake my hand, I'm gonna just...push 'em down."

"You might feel different later," I say.

"Ummph."

I wait until his breathing levels out before walking down the short hallway to the little bedroom. Robin is curled up under the giraffe sheet and when I lay down next to her, she squeaks then wraps her arm around my neck and presses her face up to the side of my head. This is how I fall asleep.

In the afternoon when we wake up, Jimmy is gone.

❧

My big check comes on Thursday, and by then I've already got my apartment picked out. It's right off of Haddon Avenue in Haddonfield, and even though most places there are kind of expensive, this one's totally in my range, with the heat and hot water included. It's not very big: there is one big room with a kitchen in it and then a little back room with a window that is totally blocked out by a big tree outside. As soon as I step into the place, I know it's meant for me. I have my checkbook with me and the landlord is only too happy to take a down payment. When I get back to my car I have to laugh out loud because this is totally like a dream come true. It's so great.

❧

Four days later, Jimmy calls home from somewhere down the Jersey shore.

"He says he got a job makin' pizzas but he'll come back to deal with the insurance stuff when it's time," Robin tells me, hanging up the phone. "I can't tell if he sounded happy or drunk."

"It was totally both."

"Oh, right."

We are sitting on the edge of the couch a little later, watching a Phillies game, when she says, "You still gonna come see me after you move into your new place?"

"Oh, yeah, absolutely," I say, meaning it.

"I don't know how to feel about you, but I know it feels good to be together."

I feel exactly the same wa,y and when her hand touches mine it starts off like a handshake but it's a long time before either one of us lets go. It's a pretty good feeling.

∞⌘∞

I get the key to the apartment on Monday. It takes me twenty minutes to move all the stuff from my car to the apartment, and I spend the next couple of hours roaming the junk shops in Collingswood, looking for furniture. I only find one small table but later on, before work, I stop and grab a futon mattress from a second-hand store in Runnemede. It takes a minute to fold it up into the trunk but once it's in and I'm back in the car, heading to the movie theater, I know I'm set.

I spend the whole night daydreaming of sleeping in my own place: *In this dream, I wake up and drink a cup of coffee while listening to the radio and thinking about the day ahead. It's just a regular day, but even though it seems normal, there's still a chance that something great might happen.*

Eventually there is a knock on the door and when I answer it, Robin is there. She's carrying a couple of books and wants to go down to the café on the corner to have breakfast. This sounds like a great idea, so I lock the door and follow her out onto the sidewalk. I'll have to go to work later but there's a lotta time before that, so almost anything could happen …

I wake up just as I'm carrying the last bag of trash out to the dumpster. The key feels weightless in my pocket, and I seriously just cannot wait to get home.

About the Author

Stephen St. Francis Decky is is a multimedia artist and writer whose work has appeared in festivals, collections, and museums internationally, including the New Britain Museum of American Art and the Museum of Fine Arts, Nagoya, Japan. As a technical collaborator, he has worked on video installations in Boston, New York, and Montana, and has taught animation and digital media courses at several schools, including Tufts University and Lycoming College. Stephen's films have screened at the Camden International Film Festival and the VOID International Animation Film Festival in Copenhagen, Denmark, among many others. He currently lives and works in upstate New York.

Enjoyed this story? Read more from Frayed Edge Press...

Literature

In Madison's Cave: A Novel by Douglas Anderson
Ambushing the Void short stories by James McAdams
¿Cómo Hacer Preguntas? or How To Make Questions: 69 Instructional Poems (in English) by Daniel Hales
Bellapalma by Jens Bjørneboe; translated by Esther Greenleaf Mürer
Ere the Cock Crows by Jens Bjørneboe; translated and with a reconstruction of the play by Esther Greenleaf Mürer
Right Guy, Wrong Time by Louise MacGregor
Stealing: A Novel in Dreams by Shelly Brivic
The Splooge Factory poety by Christina Springer

History and Politics

"Do Not Misunderstand Me": The Collected Radical Addresses to the Unity Congregation (1888-1891) by Hugh Owen Pentecost
Jeremiah Hacker: Journalist, Anarchist, Abolitionist by Rebecca Pritchard
A Nurse's Story: Medical Missionary in Korea and Siberia, 1915-1920 by Delia Battles Lewis

Street Smart Series -- Short Fiction for People on the Go

Full Fare by Jean-Bernard Pouy
Down and Out in Paris, with Cat by R.A. Bolo
The Accidental Anarchist by A.R. Melnik
Stealing MacGuffin by Matthew Kastel
Pele's Domain by Albert Tucher
"Make the Bear Be Nice" by Stephen St. Francis Decky
The Day is Gone by Shelonda Montgomery

Visit us at: https://www.frayededgepress.com/